JAPANESE URBAN LEGENDS

By Roberta Merli

Copyright © 2017 Roberta Merli
All rights reserved
Cover image: © Captblack76 | Dreamstime.com

Table of contents

Introduction 5

The purple mirror 7

The white string 9

Kuchisake-onna 11

Toire no Hanako 15

Aka Manto 19

Teke Teke 23

Gozu – Cow's head 27

The Red Room 31

The Kiyotaki tunnel 33

Kagome, Kagome 35

The Himuro Palace 39

The Inunaki village 41

Hitori Kakurenbo 43

Hyakumonogatari Kaidankai 47

Tomino's hell 49

School at night 51

Cursed Kleenex commercial 53

The curse of the Colonel 55

Okiku the doll 57

Jinmenken 59

The ghost passenger 61

The slit girl 63

Conclusion 65

Introduction

Japan is a land rich in folklore and the mythology of this country is really vast. With the passing of time, however, traditional myths and legends have become more modern; other legends, instead, were born in modern times to exorcise man's new fears. The latter are called urban legends.
Today, thanks also to more accessible media and social media, these new legends can spread to millions of people very quickly, thanks to credible situations, the fear that the facts told in the legend will happen to us and the timeless formula of those who tell them: "The friend of a friend of mine told me that...". In this way we feel the story as close and potentially dangerous for us, leading us to believe these bizarre stories even when reason tells us that they cannot be true. I mean, it's not true, but I believe it.

Urban legends are present in every country and similarities can often be found between urban legends of different countries. Japan, however, as often happens, manages to give each of its stories, tales or legends a particular aura that stimulates the curiosity of us westerners.
In this book, I will present some of the most disturbing Japanese urban legends, from the most well-known to the darkest and less known.

JAPANESE URBAN LEGENDS

The purple mirror

It is said that a few years ago, in Japan, a girl received a mirror as a gift from her mother. The girl, who was very vain, was very happy with that gift and always looked at her own reflection. She began to want to be more and more beautiful and thinner and thinner, until she fell into the trap of anorexia. Every day she became thinner and thinner, white and weaker, but looking in her mirror she always looked beautiful and prosperous. One day, she wanted to decorate her mirror and decided to color it purple. After this decoration, however, the girl began to see herself for what she was: a pale, sickly skeleton. The young girl became furious at that sight and threw the mirror to the ground, shattering it, but she immediately regretted it. Shortly afterwards it would have been her twentieth birthday, but she never celebrated it because she was hit by a car and killed almost instantly. Her last words were:

"Purple mirror... purple mirror... purple mirror... purple mirror...".

The parents searched for the purple mirror in the girl's room, in vain. Young people in the area started talking about her death and rumors about the girl began to spread all over the country. Shortly after her death, many young people began to die in strange circumstances, all of them at the age of 20. There were two mysterious facts surrounding these sinister deaths: one was that the cause of death could not be established with certainty, while the second was that pieces of purple glass were always found in their rooms.

From that moment on, the words "purple mirror" are considered cursed. Legend has it that anyone who remembers them on their 20th birthday dies. These words are a danger to all those under the age of twenty; if you have not yet turned twenty, forget this story and these cursed words, don't think about this sentence anymore and take the image of the purple mirror out of your head. Your life depends on it.

The white string

In the 80s, in Japan, a girl wanted to get her ears pierced, but her parents thought she was too young and prevented her from doing so. She begged them every day, because all her classmates had had their ears pierced and she was the only one who hadn't. She begged and begged her parents until they, exasperated, decided to agree. They gave her money so that she could go to the jewelry store at the mall and get the longed-for piercing. She decided to keep the money to herself and have her earlobes pierced by a classmate. The latter took a pin and sterilized it with a flame, then pierced her friend's earlobes. Everything seemed to go smoothly, but a few days later, the girl started to feel an itch in her ear during class. It was a persistent itch, accompanied by pain. She decided to go to the bathroom to check and she saw that one of her lobes was swollen and red. She kept scratching until she noticed a white string sticking out of the lobe, just where it was pierced. She tried to remove it, but this little white string seemed to be endless, so she decided to cut it. After cutting it, all went black: the girl had gone blind. She was immediately taken to the hospital, where she was told she would never regain her sight. That white string she had cut was in fact her optic nerve.

Kuchisake-onna

Kuchisake-onna is a Japanese legend about a woman who lived hundreds of years ago, perhaps in the Heian period (8th to 12th century). This woman was the wife of a samurai and it is said to be beautiful and very vain. The young woman, however, was unfaithful to her husband, who one day discovered her affair and, in a fit of rage, struck her with his katana making a cut on her face that went from ear to ear, opening her mouth completely. The man then shouted at her: "Who's going to tell you that you're beautiful now?"

The urban legend about Kuchisake-onna

Over the years, then, in Japan, the rumor began to spread that a woman with a surgical mask, very common in Japan for smog and fear of disease, stopped passers-by asking them:

"Am I beautiful?"

The passerby usually answered affirmatively, then the woman took off her mask, revealing her disfigured face and devouring the unfortunate man with her huge mouth.

Other versions say that after taking off the mask, the woman chased the passers-by to kill them on their doorstep. The only way to escape her seems to be to confuse her with your answer, so that you have time to escape. It is also said that throwing fruit or candies at her will distract her as she stops to pick them up and eat them. In 1979, also in Japan, other rumors about kuchisake-onna spread. Many complains were made about a woman with her mouth covered by a mask who stopped the students asking them:

"Am I beautiful?".

If they said yes, the woman would take off her mask, asking the question again. If the unlucky studen answered "no", he would be murdered with a pair of scissors and if he answered "yes" he would be disfigured too. Here, too, the best strategy seems to be to answer confusedly and then run away. These rumors shook the Japanese so much that the youngest students were accompanied home in groups by a teacher. Finally, in the 2000s, the urban legend spread to other parts of Asia such as South Korea.

The latest version may have originated from a real incident happened in 1970 in Japan, when a woman who was chasing children was hit by a car and her face was disfigured with a cut on her face.

Toire no Hanako

Toire no Hanako ("Hanako of the toilet") is a Japanese urban legend, present in every prefecture of the country. This legend is about the spirit of a little girl, Hanako, who haunts elementary school bathrooms. This urban legend went viral in the 1990s but is thought to date back to the 1950s. There are various versions depending on the area, but the most common is the following: Toire no Hanako was the spirit of a little girl, with a bob haircut and wearing a red skirt, who was killed by her parents, or who died during a World War II bombing, or who committed suicide in the school bathroom. Anyway, it seems to haunt the third cabin of the girls' bathroom on the third floor. It seems to be a benign spirit and some say it protects the school from evil ghosts. If you want to avoid her anyway, just stay away from the third bathroom cubicle on the third floor or, once you meet her, just show her the good grades you got at school and she will disappear.

According to another version, if you knock three times at the cubicle and ask "Hanako, are you there?" you'll hear a voice saying "Yes, I'm here", then the door opens and Hanako drags you into the toilet with her, straight to hell.

Another version says that Hanako appears when you run out of toilet paper, asking "do you want red toilet paper or blue toilet paper?". If you choose the first one you will meet a violent death, if you choose the second one you will meet a death by strangulation or bleeding. Some students were so scared of it that they had problems with their bladder because they refused to go to the bathroom during school hours.

Another urban legend says that the spirit that haunts the school toilet is that of a boy named Yousuke and that, once invoked, a bloody hand comes out of the toilet. Another one tells of the spirit of a girl without lower limbs who haunts the toilets looking for her legs.

Several movies were made about Hanako-San in Japan, three in the 1990s and one in 2013.

The origin

Toire no Hanako is not the only Japanese legend set in a bathroom. This phenomenon stems from the belief that spirits, if present in a house, are holed up in the smallest room, the bathroom. This may be due to the ancient superstition that wells were inhabited by spirits and with the advent of modernity the well was replaced by the toilet.

Moreover, in Japan, again for reasons of superstition, toilets are always located in the darkest part of a house, making them more scary.

Aka Manto

Aka Manto is a supernatural being protagonist of a Japanese urban legend dating back a few decades ago and set,again, in school bathrooms.

The legend of Aka Manto ("red cloak"), like all urban legends, is told with some variations depending on the place. It is about a ghost who appears in the toilets, especially those of schools, and asks questions to those who are using the toilet. It usually appears in the fourth compartment of the bathroom, because the number 4, in Japan, is associated with death. In one version the ghost asks:

"Do you want the red toilet paper or the blue toilet paper?"

If you answer "red", you'll be stabbed to death and your clothes will turn red with your blood. If you answer "blue", you'll be strangled until your face turns blue.

Other versions of punishment include being skinned alive (if you answer "red"), bleed to death (if you answer "blue"), or changing your skin color permanently depending on your answer.

Other versions of the question may be:

"Red cape or blue cape?"

"Red hand or blue hand?"

"Red tongue or blue tongue?"

As we have seen, answering with one of two possibilities given by Aka Manto results in a horrible death. But what happens if you try to answer another color? Unfortunately, in this case you will be swallowed up by the earth and end up in the underworld. Some versions, however, predict that if you answer "yellow", Aka Manto will stick your head in the cup, but will not kill you (while others claim that she will stick your head in the toilet until you drown. So, answer "yellow" at your own risk!). In case Aka Manto asks you:

"Do you want the red toilet paper or the white one?"

Know that if you answer "red" a tongue will come out of the toilet and lick your bottom, while if you answer "white" a hand will come out of the toilet and hit you on the bottom. In the rare case that the question includes "purple toilet paper" choose that one, because it is the only option that will allow you to escape. Some witnesses say that even answering "I don't want any paper" will allow you to escape.

Origins of Aka Manto

The entity Aka Manto in the legend is a ghost or spirit wearing a red cloak and a white mask. But whose ghost? Some versions say it's the spirit of an extremely handsome boy. So handsome that he swept all the girls off his feet. So wonderful was his charm that some girls fainted just by looking at him. The story goes that one day this boy kidnapped a girl and they never heard from them again. Other sources claim that he is not a ghost, but a serial killer hiding in toilets. We have news of the legend of Aka Manto since the early '30s, where the word "cape" designated a particular kimono, while today it is used to indicate a cloak. So, depending on the generation, people imagine Aka Manto dressed in different ways. The meaning of this legend is not clear. Since it materializes in the school bathrooms, perhaps it serves to represent the anxiety of the students who are put under pressure with a question that is impossible to answer correctly.

Note that Aka Manto is not the only Japanese urban legend that takes place in a toilet, such as the previous Toire no Hanako.

Teke Teke

Teke teke is the spirit of a girl with her body cut in half. The legend that's passed down is that of a little boy who was on his way home from school. The boy had stayed at school after class to do extracurricular activities, as is customary in Japan, and when he was about to return home it was already dark. He had decided to avoid the larger streets, preferring a longer but quieter internal path between the neighborhoods of his city. As he walked through this maze of streets and houses, he had the feeling that he was being watched. He tried not to pay attention to that strange feeling, but despite his efforts the fear of being observed came back stronger than before.

The little boy was very frightened and accelerated his pace, afraid to even turn around. Then, he found himself in a clearing surrounded by houses he did not recognize. He must have taken a wrong turn and now he didn't know where he was. From the windows of one of these houses he noticed a girl with her elbows leaning against the windowsill. He approached the house to ask her for information and as he got closer, he could see more and more details. The girl seemed to be about his age and she was smiling. The closer he got, however, the more the girl's expression changed, turning into a rabid grin. The boy didn't have the time to ask himself why this change happened, for the girl jumped out of the window and stood in front of him. What the boy saw left him breathless.

The girl in front of him had no legs. It was a torso that moved using its hands or elbows, and when it moved it made a strange "teke-teke-teke-teke" sound. The little boy, after a moment of confusion, began to run. As he ran, he could hear the creature behind him: teke-teke-teke-teke. But he didn't have the courage to turn around. Suddenly, he found himself in a dead end. He turned and saw the creature in front of him. The fear was too strong and the boy fainted. The next morning, a young boy was found dead in a dead end. His body had been cut in two and the only clues were the prints of two hands approaching the body.

Origin of the legend

Legend has it that in 1969 a girl committed suicide because of bullying, by throwing herself on the tracks a few seconds before the train arrived. The girl's body was cut in half by the train that couldn't stop in time. After her death, the girl became a vengeful spirit (an onryo) and vented her revenge against those who resemble the people who drove her to suicide. She carries a scythe and cuts her victims in two.

There are other versions of the legend, in which the protagonist is a nurse, or a girl who is killed or dies as a result of an accident. The result is the same: the protagonist loses her legs and takes revenge by cutting her victims in two.

Moral of the legend

Initially, the legend was to prevent children and teenagers from venturing near the stations at night, for the teke teke struck near the place of her death. In the following years the legend changed and teke teke no longer struck in stations, but in schools and especially in toilets. In the new versions, teke teke has a name, Kashima Reiko, and will ask you where her legs are. The correct answer is "at Meishin station". If you answer incorrectly, you will be killed with her scythe. She may even ask you who told you where her legs are and you will have to answer "Kashima Reiko". But be careful! If dhe asks you what her name is, you won't answer "Kashima Reiko", but "Mask, Death, Demon". This is because the name "Kashima" is an abbreviation of the words Kamen (mask), Shinin (dead person) and Ma (demon).

In 2009, the film "Teke Teke" was released, followed by "Teke Teke 2".

I'm also sorry to tell you that now that you've read his story, teke teke can appear in your bathroom within a month. Good luck and remember to answer the questions correctly!

Gozu – Cow's head

This urban legend tells of a story so frightening that it kills anyone who listens to it. The story, known only as "Cow's head", was discovered in the 17th century, but its origins remain a mystery. According to the legend, there are several written testimonies of the time that attest the existence of a story called "Cow's head", but the story itself is lost, or rather, have been destroyed. The writings that mention it describe it as a terrible tale, so frightening that it would kill anyone who listens to it. Almost all of its copies, therefore, have been burned to avoid further victims. However, some copies escaped this fate and were fragmented and then scattered all over Japan. That's why the details of the story are unknown, because whoever listens to it will die of fear shortly afterwards, following violent chills.

It is said that one day, an elementary school teacher had come into possession, somehow, of a copy of this story. During class trips, he used to tell scary stories to the kids on the bus to keep them busy so they wouldn't make too much noise. One day, on a field trip, he decided to tell the story of the cow's head. As soon as he started to tell it, his students turned pale, begging the teacher to stop. The teacher, however, seemed not to listen to their requests and continued to tell the story, as if he were possessed by a mysterious force. The man will only remember that he came to his senses a little later, to find himself in the remains of the bus that had had an accident, ending up in a ditch. Both the pupils and the driver were dead, all with a strange foam coming out of their mouths. The teacher never told the story of the cow's head again.

On some websites there is a version of the deadly story, which I will report below.

It is said that Gozu's story originated in the Meiji period, which runs from 1868-1912 and therefore contradicts the version that the story was already knew in the 17th century. According to this version, it all began when a representative of the emperor went to a village to make a census. The village was deserted, without any person but full of what looked like animal bones. The official then went to the nearby village, where he stayed at an inn. Intrigued by the deserted village, the man asked the innkeeper what had happened. He answered that a short time before there had been a famine and that the inhabitants of that village, desperate, had resorted to cannibalism, killing each other. Once the census had also been carried out in the second village, the official returned to the capital and wanted to verify the story told by the innkeeper. The story of the famine coincided, but the man discovered something else: the people of the second village he visited, also had a role in that macabre story. In fact, it was the inhabitants of that village who had eaten those of the first village and still had the custom of making sacrifices. The chosen person would have to wear a cow mask to look less human and make the task easier for the torturers who would kill and eat him so as not to starve to death.

The Red Room

The red room is a fairly recent urban legend and the main version is as follows.

A student was with some of his friends, when someone asked him if he knew the "red room", a strange pop-up. He answered that he didn't know it, but being an internet fanatic, he went straight home to look for it himself. After looking for it for a while, the mysterious pop-up appeared on his PC screen. It was a small window with a completely red background on which was written, in Japanese characters "do you like it?" The boy closed the window, but it appeared again. The student closed it and closed it again, but the pop-up kept appearing and each time he had an extra word, until the sentence "do you like the red room?" was formed. The boy could also hear the voice of a child repeating the question, even though his computer was set to mute. At that point, the whole screen turned black and a list of names appeared. As he scrolled through it, he noticed that the last name was that of the boy who had told him about the red room that same afternoon. Soon after, he lost consciousness. The next day his classmates did not see him at school and after class they were told the terrible news: their friend had committed suicide and had painted the walls of his room red, using his own blood.

Legend has it that if you look for the red room, on the internet you might actually come across it.

The Kiyotaki tunnel

This urban legend is about a tunnel that still exists in Japan, the Kiyotaki tunnel. This structure was built in 1929 and it is said that its original length was 444 meters, while today the tunnel measures about 320 meters. Just this detail alone would send chills down the spine of everyone in Japan: there, in fact, the number four is associated with death. In Japanese this number can be pronounced both *yon* and *shi* and this last variant is very similar to the pronunciation of a kanji which means *death*. But that's not all: the place where the tunnel was built had already been, in the Namboku period (1336-1392), the scene of bloody battles in which many people lost their lives in a violent way; the place then became a cemetery for all the nameless soldiers.

The fear for this tunnel came to life again in the 1990s, precisely in 1998, when a girl was found hanged inside it. Now there are those who say that inside the tunnel you can hear women moaning, sometimes crying. Or that you can see the ghost of a woman or one of the many workers who died during the construction of the tunnel. There is even a legend about the traffic light at its entrance. The tunnel is in fact an alternate one-way and the traffic light helps to channel the cars from both directions. But beware: according to the legend, if you arrive in front of the tunnel and find the green light, you should stop and wait for it to turn red. Only after the green light has gone on again is it safe to pass. This is because the previous green light could be the trick of a ghost who wants to let you in and then torment you or make you have an accident. This belief is so ingrained that even today it is not uncommon to see cars standing still, waiting for the red light to go on. If instead we see in the mirror on the side of the road, of those that help the view, the face of a woman, then great misfortune will happen to us within 4 days.

Kagome, Kagome

Kagome, Kagome is the name of a game named after the nursery rhyme of the same name. One child stands still with his eyes closed, while the others circle around him and sing the nursery rhyme. At the end of the nursery rhyme, the child in the center must be able to catch the child standing behind him.
The text of the nursery rhyme varies slightly from region to region, but the meaning is always the same and a translation is as follows:

"Kagome kagome / The bird is in the basket
When, oh when will it come out?
On the night of dawn
The crane and the turtle slide
Who's in front of your back?"

Many interpretations have been given to this nursery rhyme given the ambiguity of the sentences, the punctuation and the different meanings that can be attributed to words in Japanese depending on the kanji with which they are written. The urban legend I am about to tell, however, has nothing to do with the meaning of this little song.

It is said that during the Second World War, the Germans wanted to carry out experiments to make man immortal by turning off his "death switch".

They decided to do it outside Germany and a team of doctors settled in an orphanage in Japan. Scientists began experimenting on children's brains to make them immortal, failing each time and killing the subject. It is said that the diaries of a doctor who worked in the orphanage, located near Hiroshima, have been found, and that you can read some notes about the operated children who didn't die. According to him, the children who survived the experiments seemed to forget things, seemed to have their heads in the clouds and knew things they should not have known. As an example, the doctor writes that one of the children knew what his grandmother had left him. They also often played a game that, translated, meant "around you, around you" (kagome, kagome), but their faces seemed to warp as they played it. As the end of the war approached, the Germans left the orphanage and were approached, before they left, by one of the teachers of the facility, who asked them to play one last time with the children. The game would be Kagome kagome, but the doctors, frightened by the children's expressions, fled. The urban legend goes on saying that today, visiting Hiroshima, it is possible to walk in its woods through different paths. However, if you choose a path with truck tire tracks, you can end up in a place where the orphanage where the experiments were carried out stands out. Upon entering, a teacher will welcome you and ask you if you want to play a game. If you say no, all the doors will close behind you, preventing you from escaping. If you manage to escape before the door closes, a child's spirit will follow you and you will be doomed. If you say "I don't know", all the children will start shouting in inhuman voices, "Make up your mind! Make up your mind!" If you say yes, they will make you sit on the floor and all the children will circle around you. Unfortunately, no one has ever survived to tell what happens next. The only way to survive would seem to be to answer, genuinely, "I don't know". In this case the teacher will tell you to go back to your school and watch the children play.

The Himuro Palace

This urban legend is about a strange ritual carried out by a family in his mansion: the Himuro palace. The family who lived there claimed, for generations, that the house had a portal from which evil forces would emerge.
In order to avoid this misfortune, it was necessary to perform a strange ritual, called the strangulation ritual, in which they had to take a newborn girl and raise her in total secrecy to prevent her from developing ties with the outside world.
Once the day of the ritual arrived, the girl was tied to her wrists and ankles with ropes, the ends of which were then tied to four oxen or horses.
At a certain order, the animals began to pull each one in a different direction, thus tearing the poor victim apart.
The ropes with which she was tied were then impregnated with her blood and placed over the portal, so as to prevent the evil forces from coming to Earth.
One day, however, something went wrong: one of the girls chosen for the ritual somehow met a boy and fall in love with him.
This formed a bond with the outside world, making the girl unusable for the ritual. In this way the Himuros would bring shame and disgrace to the family name. That's why the head of the family

decided to eliminate all members of the Himuro family, killing them with a katana and then taking his own life. A total of seven people died. Now there are those who say that this house, which is in a forest outside of Tokyo, is cursed by the evil forces that came out of the portal, which remained open due to the failure of the ritual.

The Inunaki village

Unlike many places at the center of urban legends, this one really exists. This is the Inunaki village, located at the foot of the mountain of the same name. Its name means "the cry of the dog" and is itself the result of a legend. It is said that a hunter was returning home after a hunting trip with his dog. When the animal started barking ferociously, the man became so nervous that he killed it. Shortly afterwards, however, he was attacked and killed by a dragon; that was why the dog was barking so insistently just before, he wanted to warn him of the danger.

This is the legend of the name of this village, but recently another legend originated about its nature. It is said that this village is isolated from everything and that Japanese law has no effect there. There are also signs at the gates of the village, warning potential explorers: "Japanese law has no effect in this village".

Legend has it that any kind of crime can be committed in the village of Inunaki. From theft to murder, to incest, everything is allowed in this remote Japanese village. It is also said that there is a maniac inside it, who kills visitors who venture into the village with an axe.

Other versions of the legend speak instead of a mysterious disease, a plague that decimated the population until it was completely eliminated, making Inunaki a ghost village.

What's true about these legends? We have already ascertained that the village really exists, but is it really inhabited by ruthless murderers who are not afraid of Japanese law?
The answer is no: the village of Inunaki was a coal-producing area in the early 1900s and until the Second World War, then it was gradually abandoned. In 1986 a dam was built on the site, called the Inunaki Dam.

The origin of this urban legend, however, probably stems from something that actually happened. In 1938, a 21-year-old man named Mutsuo Toi killed 30 of his villagers using a rifle, a katana and an axe. The fact is known as the Tsuyama Massacre.

Hitori Kakurenbo

Everyone knows the game of hide-and-seek and everyone has played it at least once, but what I will explain now is a scary variation: hide-and-seek alone.
Born as a fashion in Japan and called "Hitori Kakurenbo" it soon became famous in other parts of the world, often with chilling consequences.

Here are the rules:
- Don't let the game last more than two hours, it could get too dangerous.
- When you play, you must be the only human beings in the house.
- When you're hiding, you have to remain absolutely silent
- Under no circumstances at all will you come out of your hiding place before your time.

Required items:
- A rag doll with arms and legs
- Rice enough to fill the puppet
- A nail clipper
- Needle and long red thread
- A knife or scissors
- A bathtub (alternatively, a sink is fine)
- A cup of water and salt

Preparation:

Using the knife or scissors, open the rag doll and remove the stuffing. Fill the puppet with rice, cut a nail and put it together with the rice inside the puppet. Sew the puppet with the red thread and then, without cutting it, wrap the puppet with the same thread. Fill the bathtub or sink with water, give the doll a name that is different from your name, for example "Teddy" and start the game.

The game:

The game must start at exactly 3:00 AM. On the third chime, take Teddy to the bathroom and place him on the edge of the previously filled tub, hold him tight and, watching him, repeat three times: "I'm on this round!"
After the third time, throw Teddy in the bathtub, get out of the bathroom, close the door and turn off all the lights in the house. Pick a wall that acts as a home base and slowly count to 10.
When you're done, take the knife or scissors, go back to the bathroom and get Teddy, shout "I found you, Teddy!" and release him from the red wire you tied him up with. Now yell, "Teddy, now it's your turn," and put him back in the tub.
Pick a hiding place, take the saltwater cup and take it with you without spilling the contents. Never.

Stay in your hiding place without making a sound, control your breathing too. Do not leave for any reason in the world, no matter what you hear. You may hear footsteps, whispers, voices, but for God's sake don't go out and don't pour the water! Stay hidden until dawn, then you can end the game like this: take a sip of salt water and hold it in your mouth, don't spit it out! Run to the bathroom and look for Teddy. He may not be in the tub anymore, so you'll have to look for him and find him. Absolutely.

Once you find him, spit out the water in your mouth and then pour the water from the cup over him and yell "I won!" three times. Actually, you *almost* won.

Now you're gonna have to dry Teddy off and then burn him completely. Once he's completely burned, then yes, you win. However, it is possible that in the following weeks you may hear strange presences in the house, voices calling you, hands grabbing you, and sudden chills.

The rice inside the puppet serves to attract the spirits, while the red thread symbolizes the blood vessels. Play hide-and-seek alone at your own risk.

Hyakumonogatari Kaidankai

The name of this game literally means "set of one hundred fantastic stories" and was very popular in Japan in the Edo Period (1603-1868).
It is thought that this game originated as a test of courage for the samurai and had very specific rules. The test took place in three adjacent rooms so as to form an L if seen from above. In the last room, 100 blue lanterns were lit and a mirror was placed on the floor. Those who took part in the ritual, on the other hand, had to settle in the first room. The rehearsal was to take place on a new moon night and the members had to be dressed in blue. The room in which they were had to be completely devoid of both weapons and lights. The test consisted in telling, in turn, a *kaidan* which is a ghost story. Once the story was finished, the person who had narrated it had to walk into the second room and then into the third, where he had to turn off a lamp looking in the mirror. Then, he would return to the first room, where the stories would continue until all the lamps were turned off. Once all the lamps were off, the darkness would fall and it would be possible to invoke the spirits.

The modern version

The modern version of this game can be played in one room. There must be 100 candles, preferably blue, and participants will have to take turns telling a ghost story. At the end of each story, a candle will be blown out, and after blowing out the last one, a window will open from which supernatural entities will enter.

10-stories version

This version of the game can only be played by one person. The ritual can take place in a lit room, but 10 candles are required. The person will have to tell 10 ghost stories and blow out one candle at the end of each story. Once all the candles are blown out, the narrator can see the underworld.

Tomino's hell

This is the title of a cursed poem, which was published in 1919 by the poet Saizo Yaso, in a collection of poems. According to legend, whoever reads the poem aloud will die. The text is as follows, and although it is a translation, if you decide to read it aloud, you do so at your own risk.

" Big sister spits blood, little sister spits fire.

Sweet Tomino spits jewelry
Tomino died alone and fell into hell...

Where there aren't even flowers.
Is Tomino's older sister whipping her?

The number of red marks is worrying.
Whipped, beaten, hit.

The path to eternal hell is only one.

Ask for a guide to the dark hell,
From the golden sheep to the nightingale.

How much you put in the leather bag,
the preparations for the journey to hell.

Spring comes and in the woods and valleys,
Seven tours through the dark valley of hell.

In the cage there's a nightingale, in the cart a sheep
There are tears in sweet Tomino's eyes.

Weep, nightingale, for the woods and rain
Intoning your love for your sister.

The echo of your crying resounds in hell
And the blood red flowers bloom.

Through the seven mountains and valleys of hell,
Sweet Tomino continues her journey.

To welcome you to hell
The shimmering spikes of the needled mountain

They pierce flesh and bone,
Like a sign of sweet Tomino."

Rumor has it that someone read the English translation in a radio show called "Radio Urban Legends". At first everything was fine, but the longer he continued reading, the more he felt sick.

Halfway through the poem he felt so bad that he had to stop reading and, a few days later, he was victim of an accident that left him with seven stitches.

School at night

According to this urban legend, several years ago Japan would have found itself in need of building new schools quickly. The government decided to buy plots of land on which old, abandoned cemeteries stood, in order to pay for the land at bargain prices. Because of this choice, many Japanese schools are allegedly haunted and by going to the school at midnight it is possible to witness disturbing and frightening facts.
The most harmless include footsteps and candlelight without anyone being present at the school. One could also see a ball bouncing alone in the gym and the unlucky ones could see a severed head floating in front of them. Digging in the schoolyard, it is possible to find bones and old graves, remnants of the ancient cemetery on which the structure would have been built. Ancient buildings may also appear, but don't go near them because those who do disappear into thin air.

Cursed Kleenex commercial

It's a Kleenex commercial that aired in Japan in 1986. In the commercial you can see a woman dressed in white watching a child dressed as a Japanese ogre. She hands him a Kleenex handkerchief, then makes an affectionate gesture to the little ogre and the commercial closes with the two watching a handkerchief fly away in the breeze. There are no voices in the commercial, just a background song and it is this song that started the urban legend. The audience started claiming that the lyrics of the song were a curse in German, although the lyrics were clearly in English, and that its translation was: "Die, die, all are cursed and will die". It's actually the song "It's a Fine Day", by Jane & Barton.

Then rumors began to spread about the actors in the commercial: it was said that the child dressed as an ogre had died and that the actress, Keiko Matsuzaka, had died or was hospitalized or had given birth to an ogre child.

The curse of the Colonel

This urban legend is thought to be the cause of the defeats of Japanese baseball team Hanshin Tigers. In Japan, baseball is the most popular sport and was introduced to the country by U.S. teacher Horace Wilson in 1870.

When, in 1985, the Hanshin Tigers won the championship by surprise, their fans were seized with euphoria and went to celebrate on the Ebisubashi Bridge on the Dotonbori Canal. Fans who looked like the players were selected and one by one jumped into the canal. But there was one problem: none of the fans looked like Randy Bass, an American player. So, the fans had the brilliant idea to use the statue of Colonel Sanders, Kentucky Fried Chicken's founder, because like Bass he was not Japanese and had a beard. They took the statue from a store and threw it in the canal.

From that moment on, the team began a series not only of defeats, but of bad results that the fans attributed to Colonel Sanders. According to them, the Colonel put a curse on the team that would not stop until after his recovery from the canal. Several attempts were made, all to no avail until 2009, when divers came across the statue. Unfortunately, however, the curse has not yet been broken because the statue still lacks the glasses and the left hand.

Okiku the doll

Okiku the doll is found in a temple in Japan and is thought to contain the spirit of a little girl.
It is said that in 1918 a young man named Eikichi Suzuki bought a gift for his little two-yars-old sister Okiku, in Sapporo, Japan. He saw a doll in a shop window and thought it was the perfect gift, so he bought it. The doll was about 40 cm tall (16 inches), with black hair reaching up to her shoulders, two black beads as eyes and dressed in a traditional kimono. Okiku was very happy with the doll and always kept it with her. She played with it every day and decided to give it her name, Okiku. Unfortunately, the girl died the following year from an infection and her loved ones mourned her a lot. In Japan it is common to have an altar in the house dedicated to the dead, where is customary to put their pictures and incense to pray to them, and Okiku's parents decided to put the doll, so dear to their little girl, there too.
Soon, however, they began to notice that the doll's hair was beginning to grow. It didn't simply stretch, keeping a clean cut at the ends, but grew irregularly, just like a human being's hair. The family began to believe that their daughter's spirit had taken refuge in the doll.
In 1938, the Suzuki family moved away, but did not take the Okiku doll with them, thinking that if they removed it from their daughter's grave, the spirit

would no longer have a place to stay. So, they decided to leave it in Mannenji Temple. They informed the temple monk about Okiku's story and how her hair grew, and he, too, could see over time that it was all true: the Okiku doll's hair continued to grow. When it grew to her feet, they decided to cut it off, noticing that it was still growing. The monk then decided to cut it off every time it reached her waist.

Now, several pictures of the doll with the different haircuts can be seen near the doll itself, in the Temple, on the altar dedicated both to the Okiku girl and the Okiku doll. It is thought that the phenomenon is due to the spirit of the little girl who haunted the doll and is not evil. It is said that a hair sample has been analyzed and that the hair actually belongs to a child, but this data has not been confirmed.

Today, you can still see the doll on display in a shrine in Mannenji Temple in Iwamizawa City, Hokkaido.

Jinmenken

According to legend, the jinmenken are beings with the body of a dog and a human face. Seen from afar they look like medium-sized dogs with ruffled hair, but if you go near them you will discover a chilling detail. Their face is human. Despite the fact that, usually, the beings who inhabit Japanese folklore are malignant, it seems that the jinmenken are not. Or rather, their goal is not to kill those who meet them, nor to hurt or frighten them. If you were to come face to face with a jinmenken, the most likely thing to occur is for him to respond rudely, telling you to go away and leave him alone to mind his own business. The explanations for these kinds of sightings would be various. The most popular is that the jinmenken are the result of some secret experiment on dogs, carried out in some secret laboratory. Some of the dogs undergoing the experiments, however, would have managed to escape and reach the Japanese cities.
Another hypothesis is that the jinmenken are the manifestation of the spirits of people who died in road accidents.
Despite these modern explanations, jinmenken are popular in Japanese folklore and have been known since 1600. Their origin is probably to be found in the Japanese macaque. This macaque, in fact, has the size of a dog, a quadruped posture

but a face much more similar to the human face, rather than the muzzle of a dog.
In any case, if you should meet him, try to leave him alone.

The ghost passenger

This urban legend is also known with different variations in other parts of the world. The protagonist is an unfortunate taxi driver who, one night, gets a customer on board. He says he wants to be taken to a place the taxi driver has never heard of and proceeds to provide all the necessary information. The journey becomes long and tortuous and the mysterious passenger takes the taxi driver on a dirt road in the middle of nowhere. When the driver, confused, asks the passenger again for directions, he gets no answer; he turns to ask his client how to proceed, but discovers that there is no one in the taxi. Shocked, he looks back at the road, just in time to see that he is ending up in a ravine.

The slit girl

According to this urban legend, there is a girl, or rather a spirit in the guise of a girl, hiding in the cracks of our home. This spirit may decide to haunt a house and settle in all those cracks that may be in a house, such as between a piece of furniture and the wall or in the crack of a closet door left half open. Once it has decided which house to settle in, this spirit lets the inhabitants of the house lead their lives without disturbing them, going unnoticed. If, however, by chance, you should meet her gaze, then you could get into serious trouble. When you look at the girl in the crack, she will ask you to play hide-and-seek. In some versions, for the game to start, you'll have to accept her proposal, while in others, your consent or denial is worth absolutely nothing and the game will start when the spirit asks you the question.

Now, you may think that she has to hide while you have to look for her, but instead she has to look for you. And if she finds you, that is, if you meet her gaze again, by chance, in a crack, then the girl in the crack will drag you with her into hell.

So, my advice is to be very careful not to leave any cracks in your house: make sure you close closets, cupboards and drawers well and try not to look in the cracks that you can't cover. Your life depends on it!

Who is this girl? According to the legend it is clear that she is a spirit, but we do not know exactly whose. One of the most reliable theories is that she is a previous tenant of your house, now deceased, who does not want to leave his home.

Conclusion

Some of these urban legends may seem distant from our culture, but that is why they exert an irresistible fascination on our curiosity.

Here ends our journey through Japanese urban legends, hoping that they entertained you and, why not, even scared you a bit.

Sources

http://umaibo.net

http://danglingmouse.com

jpinfo.com

https://sugoiinipponnews.blogspot.it

Cover image: © Captblack76 | Dreamstime.com

Printed in Great Britain
by Amazon